Treasure Trolls™

Snicker Doodle

a Treasure Troll Tale

Stephen Cosgrove

illustrated by
Diana Rice Bonin

A Golden Book • New York

Western Publishing Company, Inc., Racine, Wisconsin 53404

The Carousel ® ™
13110 NE 177th PL
Woodinville, WA 98072

Publisher: Nancy L. Cosgrove
Business Director: Terri Anderson
Creative Editor: Matt Stuart

Snicker Doodle

a Treasure Troll Tale by Stephen Cosgrove

Dedicated to Opal and Al Smith, two trolls who have been a treasure to me. Thank you for being there for all the trolls.

Stephen

Magic is here – for this is the land of Hodge Podge and the village of Hairst Bree. In this land and in this village live fairylike creatures called Treasure Trolls. Their laughter tinkles like crystal bells as they scamper about searching for magical little jewels called WishStones. For every troll knows that when you wish upon a WishStone all your dreams come true. When a WishStone is found, the Treasure Troll who finds it can wish upon it. All he or she needs to say is,

"TINKLE, TWINKLE, HAIR SO FUZZY.
TINKLE, TWINKLE, BEES GO BUZZY.
WISH I MAY,
WISH I MIGHT
HAVE THE WISH I WISH TONIGHT."

And just like that the wishes are granted. Magic is here – in the very hearts of the Treasure Trolls and in the WishStones they carry.

It was a magical night in the land of Hodge Podge, for this was the night of the Midsummer Moon. When the moon is at its fullest, the Treasure Trolls find the biggest and best of the WishStones. With their lamps held high, the little trolls happily bobbed and weaved from the village of Hairst Bree. The lamps flitted and flickered like fireflies up the trail to Mount Wishbone where the WishStones were hidden.

The sweet summer night was filled with song as the trolls found one sparkling treasure after another.

Laughter and light danced all around the village, except in one old thatched-roof cottage with its windows tightly shuttered. This was the home of the two old Treasure Trolls called Trippet Snicker and Trivia Doodle. They sadly peeked through the window of the cottage and watched forlornly as the other trolls went their merry way. This was a dark sad house wherein lived very sad trolls.

But they had not always been sad. A long time ago, as young trolls with hair so wild, they had married in a bower of flowers beside the Shiver River. There they pledged their love and adoration forever. They were very happy.

Married as Trippet and Trivia Snicker Doodle, they had smiled shy Treasure Troll smiles as a springtime shower exploded into a rainbow.

It was a time of grand beginnings.

As a couple, the Snicker Doodles happily worked and played together. With trees chopped from the Shuffle Forest, they had built a cottage. Each special log had been bonded one to the other with wooden pegs until walls were formed. Later windows and doors were cut. The roof was arched with special thatch, woven from purple thistle. All was bound with dandelion stems to seal the cottage from inclement weather.

Their cottage was built at the very end of the Fluffershuffle Trail in a clearing that later became the village of Hairst Bree.

In time, Trippet and Trivia became mother and father, having bundles and bundles of Treasure Troll babies. There were always one or two Treasure Tots cradled in Trivia's arms, and three or four rocking in the limbs of a tree while Trippet held yet another.

Trippet and Trivia gave birth to what became nearly the entire population of Treasure Trolls. Triska and Trousers Teeterklunker were related to Tinkling Gigglesfooten, who was related to Trickle, who was of the Trumpetsnicker Clan, all twelve of whom were Snicker Doodles on their mother's and their father's side, too. Trounce Buttonbreaker and his little brother, Tweezer, were second cousins twice-removed to Tizzy Trudgenwalker, who was Trippet and Trivia's granddaughter through her mother, Tiny (who wasn't small at all but really rather large).

In fact, most of the Treasure Trolls that lived in the land of Hodge Podge were related to the Snicker Doodles – and if they weren't, they wished they were.

Trippet and Trivia, like all Treasure Trolls, loved to mine for the elusive WishStones. Once a year, at the time of the Midsummer Moon, they lit the wicks of their lanterns and walked arm-in-arm up the Fluffershuffle Trail to Wishbone Mountain. There, with pick and shovel, they dug in the mines, looking for the magical jewels. As they worked, they sang a gay Treasure Troll song, and like a faint, whimsical echo, the stones sang back. Every time they heard the echo, they dug furiously. Then, in a flurry of dust and dirt, Trippet and Trivia found the treasure they sought, WishStones.

What a wonderful life! How bright the land! How happy they were!

But, as of late, something had gone wrong in the village of Hairst Bree in the land of Hodge Podge. Something was sadly wrong with Trippet and Trivia Snicker Doodle!

Now, while the others sang, they mumbled. Now, when the others laughed, they grumbled. For there was no laughter in their lives anymore. Chores once done with vigor and purpose by this old couple were now left part-done and often not done at all. Wooden bowls and pewter plates were stacked high in the kitchen where Trippet normally had scrubbed everything squeaky, sparkling clean.

Now, while the other Treasure Trolls danced, they sat on sagging wicker chairs. Not only did their chairs sag, but Trippet and Trivia also seemed to sag, as they sat with heads bowed, speaking not a word to one another. There was no longer magic here. There were just two old trolls, sitting in a very dirty kitchen.

And it wasn't just the kitchen that had suffered. In the parlor there were bits of yarn and fluff that were to have been knitted into blankets, sweaters and caps. Look, there on the basket! A half-knitted silly sock that Trippet and Trivia had worked on together for years and years. Silly because there was only one sock twelve feet long and now sad, for it was unfinished and unraveling. Row by row, the yarn had begun to pull free. The floor was now strewn with things that might have been. Something was wrong here. It seemed as though something was missing.

As the days dragged on, the sadness that had overcome Trippet and Trivia had finally spilled outside their thatched cottage into the very garden itself. The Snicker Doodle garden, once the envy of all that walked by, had become choked with weeds. Flowers that once wafted sweet perfume into the village had gone to seed and now hung uncut on yellowed stalks that twisted noisily in the wind. The fence around the garden was falling down and the paint was chipped and peeling. The fruit that had ripened on the trees was now only pecked at by small, screeching birds.

Something was very wrong. Something was mysteriously missing. Oh, this was a sad place, indeed!

All of this did not go unnoticed. For the Treasure Trolls are a gentle folk that care for others as well as themselves. As the weeks passed, they watched as Trippet and Trivia withdrew into their cottage and rarely came out. They watched and wondered as the garden fell to weeds and seeds. They watched until they could watch no more.

Finally it was Tizzy, Trousers and Tweezer who decided that something must be done. Together they walked to the Snicker Doodle cottage and called to Trippet and Trivia to let them in. The old trolls shuffled to the door, grumbling, "What do you want?"

"We want to know what has happened," they said shyly. "Why has your garden gone to seed? Why has your cottage fallen into such disrepair? Why have you gone from happy to so very sad?"

The old couple stood in the shadow of all they had built and said, "We don't know. It simply seems as though something is missing, something is lost. Now we're sad because we can't remember what it was."

"Well, that's easy enough to solve," cried the little Treasure Trolls, "for we will find it!"

Tizzy, Trousers and Tweezer ran back to the village and told the others what had been said. And so it came to be that all the Treasure Trolls in the land of Hodge Podge began searching for that which was missing from the Snicker Doodles' lives.

There was only one little problem — nobody knew *what* was missing, so they didn't know what to find. If the trolls are anything, they are an inventive lot, and so they found everything. They found buttons and bones and beetles and balls and bells and whistles. They found this and that and stuff and things. All that they found they took to the cottage, which by this time had acquired quite a pile of lost junk, much of which should never have been found.

Each item was carefully examined by the old couple, but each time they sadly shook their heads. "No," they said with a sigh, "that's not what we lost. That's not what's missing." The sadness continued for the sweet old Snicker Doodles.

Each day and each night Trippet and Trivia sat in their wicker chairs, searching through lost thoughts and dreams for the *something* that was missing in their lives.

Finally, as the pile of lost and found grew into a mountain of junk, Trippet and Trivia, hand-in-hand, sadly walked away from it all. They walked up the Fluffershuffle Trail across the Wibble-Wobble-Hobble-Quick Bridge and out into Gossamer Downs. Near the spot where they had been married years and years before, they sat upon a great rock. They sat for the longest of times and gazed into the crystal waters of the Shiver River. Single lonely tears traced down their cheeks and fell into the water. *Plip! Plop! Plip! Plop!* The tears formed circles on the surface of the water, racing out and out until they were no more.

It was quite by chance that Trippet and Trivia looked down beneath the surface of the water. There, shimmering with a red glow, were two ruby-red stones. Even as sad as they were, Trippet and Trivia knew that these stones were special indeed, for these were magical WishStones.

Carefully, Trivia rolled up his trousers and Trippet lifted her skirt as they stepped into the icy waters of the Shiver River. They forded together to the spot where they had spied the WishStones. Carefully, they each reached into the water and plucked a WishStone from the river. But these were not mere WishStones. They were WishHearts, the most magical of all the WishStones. WishHearts fill their owner's heart with love and understanding. WishHearts are for sweethearts, young and old.

As they stood in the freezing waters of the crystal river, Trippet and Trivia looked into each other's eyes. At last they knew what had gone from their lives, what had been missing.

Together they held the WishHearts against their hearts and softly chanted, wishing for that which had been lost,

"TINKLE, TWINKLE, HAIR SO FUZZY.
TINKLE, TWINKLE, BEES GO BUZZY.
WISH I MAY,
WISH I MIGHT
HAVE THE WISH I WISH TONIGHT.
I WISH FOR ALL, KIT AND CABOODLE.
I WISH LOVE FOR SNICKER AND DOODLE."

The WishHearts began to glow, and all was magic again as Trippet and Trivia rekindled what had been lost in their lives. For what Trippet and Trivia had lost – what makes relationships ever strong – was love.

Even now, all of the Treasure Trolls are wishing on their WishStones that your wishes will come true, too.

Stephen Edward Cosgrove

...was born July 26, 1945, in Spokane, Washington.

...was raised in Boise, Idaho.

...has written and published over two hundred children's titles.

...lives now with his beloved wife Nancy, his delightful stepson Matthew, his little dog Rhubarb, Snickers the attack cat and two goldfish the size of whales in the foothills just outside Seattle, Washington.